Puffy snowflakes swirl down and disappear in the cold sea.

Far from the mainland, through the snow, a small island appears. It is early December. Soon it will be . . .

CHRISTMAS ON AN ISLAND

GAIL GIBBONS

MORROW JUNIOR BOOKS
NEW YORK

To all my friends on Matinicus, many merry Christmas seasons.

Special thanks to Donna Rogers for her help on this book.

Watercolors, colored pencils, and India ink were used for the full-color illustrations.
The text type is 18-point Garamond Book.

Copyright © 1994 by Gail Gibbons
Printed in the United States of America.
1 2 3 4 5 6 7 8 9 10

Library of Congress Cataloging-in-Publication Data
Gibbons, Gail.
Christmas on an island/by Gail Gibbons.
p. cm.
Summary: Describes the way residents of a small island celebrate Christmas.
ISBN 0-688-09678-6 (trade)—ISBN 0-688-09679-4 (library)
[1. Christmas—Fiction. 2. Islands—Fiction.] I. Title. PZ7.G33914Ch 1994
[E]—dc20 93-50111 CIP AC

The small island community is mostly made up of hardy lobster fishermen and their families. Onshore the snow gets deeper. Christmas is almost here.

Some folks are busy making gifts. Inside his workshop a fisherman puts finishing touches on a toy lobster boat. In a cozy house someone clicks knitting needles together as a mitten takes shape. At the schoolhouse it is wreath-making time. These wreaths will be given to some of the older islanders as gifts.

Down at the town landing one of the islanders holds out a hat. "Pick a name," she says. This is an old island custom. Inside the hat are slips of paper with the names of everyone who will be on the island Christmas Eve. Each person who reaches into the hat will give a gift to the person whose name has been drawn.

At this time of year the lights stay on later than usual at the schoolhouse. This is a tiny island school where there are a small number of students. The teacher has written a school play that the kids rehearse and rehearse. They make props and paint sets, too.

As Christmas draws near the children and their teacher bundle up and go out into the snow-filled woods. It's time to choose a tree for the school. "This is a dandy one!" On the other side of the island some folks cut down a tree for the Christmas Eve celebration at the church.

Back inside the schoolhouse everyone is busy making ornaments and paper chains to decorate the school tree. As they work, glitter sparkles to the floor. Bits of colored paper are everywhere. *Clip . . . clip!* Over at the church islanders drape tinsel from the big tree's branches. Boxes of ornaments have been pulled out from storage. The ornaments are carefully unwrapped and hung on the tree. Some are very old. "Look! This one is from 1933!"

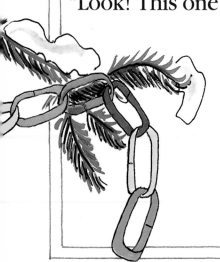

On the island there are no stores filled with holiday decorations and no grand public events to give the feeling of Christmas. The islanders must create this on their own. Down at the harbor's edge people string colored lights on trees, workshops, and some of the houses. Starting tonight, the fishing boats will have a festive harbor to return to in the dark. A fisherman hangs a wreath on his boat.

Days go by. At the town landing some islanders unload gifts they bought on the mainland. One boat tied up at the dock is called the *Sunbeam*. The people aboard this boat provide spiritual care and other services to many of the offshore islands throughout the year. Today they unload packages for the Christmas Eve celebration. Each island child will receive a gift from this organization.

Each year, it is a tradition for the island women to come together to decorate baskets and fill them with baked goods they've made. Later the baskets will be delivered to any islanders who are alone or ill this Christmas.

It's a dark and blowy night. Almost everyone who lives on the island has gathered at the schoolhouse. It's time for the Christmas play to be performed. The schoolteacher has written some very funny lines. Some of them are about things that happened on the island during the past year. Everyone laughs.

"Great play!" "Wonderful costumes!" "Isn't she cute!" The audience agrees that this is the best play ever. Someone eyes the table full of hot cider and other refreshments that will be served later on.

It's the day before Christmas. Each kitchen on the island is filled with wonderful smells from cooking and baking for tonight's big feast at the church. Gifts are wrapped. Over at the harbor friends and relatives from the mainland arrive by boat. A small plane bringing more people buzzes as it descends onto the tiny island runway.

Finally, it's Christmas Eve, time for the celebration everyone has been waiting for. Some islanders walk through the snow to the island church. Others come by car and truck. All kinds of food are carefully carried into the basement and placed on banquet tables. Other folks carry gifts upstairs to put under the tree. What a lot of commotion!

Everyone settles down. This island community has a minister in the summer months only, so today it's one of the islanders who gives a word of thanks. Then the Christmas Eve feast begins. The room fills with the sounds of everyone having a good time. "Isn't this the best ham you've ever tasted?"

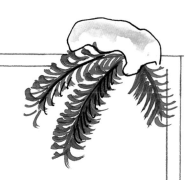

The desserts are endless—pies, cakes, lots of Christmas cookies. "What delicious pumpkin pie!" someone says, rubbing his stomach. At this small Christmas Eve gathering there is a strong feeling of friendship and warmth.

Now everyone has gone up-stairs. The scent of the Christmas tree fills the air. Hymns and carols are sung with great feeling. These islanders are very independent people who have chosen to live a rugged and sometimes dangerous life. This is a time to be grateful for the good things they have and to reflect on the meaning of Christmas.

All of a sudden, people start singing "Jingle Bells." It's the signal for Santa to come! "Merry Christmas, everyone. Ho . . . ho . . . ho!"

This year one of the fishermen is helping Santa by dressing up in his clothes. Santa is late, he tells the children, so he's filling in. He looks just like Santa, though! The kids race up the aisle to help. They take turns handing out the gifts as Santa reads the tags. "Ho . . . ho . . . This one's for Nicky!"

The Christmas tree sparkles. Santa flashes a big grin. One of the folks opens a package from her secret gift giver. "Now I wonder who this is from."

Santa is busy. More gifts are delivered by Santa's helpers. The room is filled with happy chattering. "Look what I got from the *Sunbeam*!"

Torn wrapping paper and ribbons are scattered all over the place. Cameras flash. One lone gift rests under the tree. "And who could this be for?" It's been a big night, and everyone is looking a little sleepy.

The islanders gather up their belongings to begin the trek home. Outside the wind is blowing, and it is snowy and cold. The lighthouse flashes in the distance.

It is silent on the island except for the ringing of the harbor bell. It sounds as if it's ringing in Christmas Day. Some of the children leave a snack for Santa to have when he visits their homes tonight. Soon everyone is asleep.

On Christmas morning families and friends cluster around their own Christmas trees. Sometimes island life is lonely. It means a lot to the islanders to be together on this special day. There are more Christmas gifts to be opened. Look at the beautiful toy lobster boat.

Gifts of goodies are delivered between houses by the island women. Neighbors and friends stop in to say hello. A stuffed turkey is removed from the oven. Wonderful smells fill the air.

Christmas dinners take place all over the island. Around their tables islanders share stories about past Christmas celebrations. "Remember when . . . ," one of the old-timers begins.

Christmas traditions have been passed down on this tiny island for generations. For these people it is a time to be together, to share good feelings and spread Christmas cheer.

It is Christmas on an island.